WHEN I GROW UP
I Can Go
Anywhere for Jesus

Terry Whalin

Illustrated by Jim Engel

Chariot Books™
David C. Cook Publishing Co.

When you grow up, what do *you* want to do? The world is full of exciting places. You can go anywhere in the world and do anything you want to for Jesus!

Where will you go? What will you do?

When I grow up, I'll be an airplane pilot in Peru. I'll SOAR and SWOOP through the clouds in my little airplane. I'm going to ZOOOOM over high mountains where there aren't any roads for cars or trucks.

My airplane will take missionaries to far-off places
where they can tell people about Jesus. I could fly
Bibles, goats, ropes, or even paddles for boats
in my plane. Why, I'll carry anything from pigs to
presidents!

As a pilot for Jesus, I can fly anywhere.

Not me! I'm sticking right here—close to my computer. You can't run a computer in the middle of nowhere. Where would I get batteries? Or a place to plug it in?

I'm staying close to home!

When I grow up, I want to teach missionary kids in Papua New Guinea. I'll RAP, RAP, RAP my ruler to get the kids' attention. During our school pet show, my students won't have many dogs and cats.

Instead they'll bring in snakes and rhinoceros beetles—and maybe bats!

For something special, we'll camp outside and sleep under the stars. When we swim in the river, we'll keep a sharp lookout for crocodiles!

When it's time to eat, we'll pile our food in a hole in the ground. Then we'll put hot rocks on top and cover them with leaves and a layer of dirt. Pretty soon, lunch is cooked! YUM YUM.

As a teacher for Jesus, I can go anywhere.

Forget that! Who wants to eat food buried in the dirt? Kids in other countries probably eat bugs and caterpillars!

I've heard there are zillions of languages that have never been written down. Well, maybe just thousands. The people who speak those languages don't have any books—not even the Bible. When I grow up, I'm going to be a Bible translator in Cameroon—right in the middle of Africa!

My whole family will live in a hut with mud walls like everyone else's. Maybe we'll even sleep and eat in the same hut as a local family with all their kids. Then it will be easy to learn their language.

After we can talk like the people around us, I'll write their language for them. Then I can put the Bible in their language—that's what a Bible translator does. It takes a long time to translate the Bible—even with a computer. When the people get their very own Bibles, they can learn more about Jesus.

As a Bible translator for Jesus, I can work anywhere!

Whoa, Bible translator. That sounds complicated. How can you run your computer in a mud hut?

When I grow up, I'm going to be a builder in these islands right here in the Philippines. I can pound nails with my hammer and paint walls with my paint brush and saw boards with my saw.

I'll build houses or offices or churches. I'll tell the people I'm building for Jesus!

When I buy building stuff, I'll tell people about Jesus, too. And the people will teach me just how they do things.

As a builder for Jesus, I can work anywhere.

Whew! I didn't know you could do so many things for Jesus. Maybe I could live in another country. I *could* take my computer—and lots of batteries—any place in the whole, wide world!

When I grow up, I *could* use my computer for Jesus.

I can help the Bible translators translate the Bible faster with my computer. The computer can make sure they don't miss anything—like if a verse is missing, my computer can tell. Or if something goes wrong with the computer, I can fix it!

As a computer person for Jesus, I can work anywhere.

What exciting lives you'll have when you grow up!
And no matter where you go, or whatever you do, *you*
can help people learn about Jesus.

When you follow Jesus, you can do many
different jobs—anywhere in the world!